The Christmas Story

Cinderella • Kaye Umansky
Beauty and the Beast • Jacqueline Wilson

Published 1996 by
A & C Black (Publishers) Limited
35 Bedford Row, London WC1R 4JH

ISBN 0-7136-4387-0

Text copyright © David Wood 1996
Illustrations © Asun Balzola 1996

The right of David Wood to be identified as author of this work
has been asserted by him in accordance with the Copyright,
Designs and Patents Act 1988.

A CIP catalogue record for this book is
available from the British Library.

Series Advisor: Prue Goodwin,
          Reading and Language Information Centre,
          The University of Reading.

Photoset in New Century Schoolbook.

Printed in Great Britain by
Hillman Printers (Frome) Ltd, Frome, Somerset.

Performance
A single public performance within a school of **The Christmas
Story** may be made without applying for permission, provided
that no charge, either voluntary or compulsory, is made for
attendance.

For permission to give two or more public performances of
The Christmas Story within a school or to give a public
performance of the play within a school at which an admission
charge is made, please write to Samuel French Limited,
52 Fitzroy Street, London W1P 6JR.

The Christmas Story

David Wood

Illustrated by Asun Balzola

A & C BLACK • LONDON

Contents

A Letter from the Playwright

Primary schools have traditionally produced a nativity play. A great deal of hard work is usually put in by staff, parents and the children themselves. For the children it is often their first opportunity to dress up and appear on stage, helping them to develop their self-confidence and to work together towards the excitement of a performance.

This version of the nativity story was written at the request of several teachers who wanted a play which revealed the human side of the great event. I have tried to combine the traditional elements of the holy story with reverent humour, giving Joseph the narration. Joseph, at first surprised and hurt by Mary's news, accepts it, and gives her great support. His reaction is a personal one, in contrast with the wider reaction to Christ's birth symbolised by the sophisticated Three Kings and the unworldly shepherds. The Angel Gabriel co-ordinates the event, which culminates in the traditional tableau in the stable.

The main characters offer good acting opportunities and the actors playing them will have to learn a fair amount of dialogue. But there are many other middle-sized parts. And lots of walk-on parts for younger children! One of the actors is required to sing solo, but most of the singing is led by a choir. I have assumed that a teacher will accompany the carols on the piano or a guitar, but an orchestra would be an exciting thought! All the sound effects can be made using percussion instruments.

The Christmas carols and hymns have been chosen to develop the action of the story, in the same way that the songs in a musical do. The intention is not that the actors should stop for the choir to sing a carol and then recommence the play. The intention is that the lines that are sung should be an integral part of the whole drama in the same way as the lines that are spoken. I realise that the director of this play may want to add more carols, or to substitute others. Please feel free to do so, but be assured they will be most effective if they relate closely to the action of the story.

I have included an interval, to give everyone a short rest and to allow the audience to have a cup of coffee! But it is perfectly acceptable to perform the play straight through, simply by cutting the short Joseph and Mary scene before the interval.

I do hope you will enjoy it!

Characters in Order of Appearance

Mary
Joseph

The Three Kings: Caspar
                     Melchior
                     Balthazar

First Shepherd
Second Shepherd
Shepherd Boy
Sheep

Gabriel
Angels

Cows
Donkey

The Roman Soldiers: First Soldier
                       Second Soldier
                       Third Soldier
                       Fourth Soldier

First Innkeeper
Second Innkeeper
Third Innkeeper
Fourth Innkeeper
Fifth Innkeeper

Voices from the Inn (these could be played by members of the choir.)

Last Innkeeper
Innkeeper's Wife

Choir
Sound Effects Makers / Percussion Instrumentalists

List of Scenes and their Locations

Act 1

Scene 1 – The Nativity Tableau   : *Inside the Stable*
Scene 2 – Gabriel's Visitation   : *Mary's Garden*
Scene 3 – The Roman Soldiers' Proclamation : *Mary and Joseph's House*
Scene 4 – The Three Kings See the Star   : *The Kings' Observatory*
Scene 5 – While Shepherds Watched   : *On a Hillside*

[Interval if desired]

Act 2

Prologue – On the Road

Scene 1 – The Tax Gathering in Bethlehem   : *The Roman Soldiers' Office*
Scene 2 – No Room at the Inn   : *Outside the Tavern*
Scene 3 – Jesus is Born   : *Inside the Stable*
Scene 4 – The Travellers Arrive   : *Inside the Stable*

List of Carols

Verses and fragments of the following Christmas hymns and carols are sung:

Silent Night

While Shepherds Watched Their Flocks By Night

We Three Kings of Orient Are

The First Nowell

O Little Town of Bethlehem

Away In a Manger

O Come, All Ye Faithful

Hark! The Herald Angels Sing

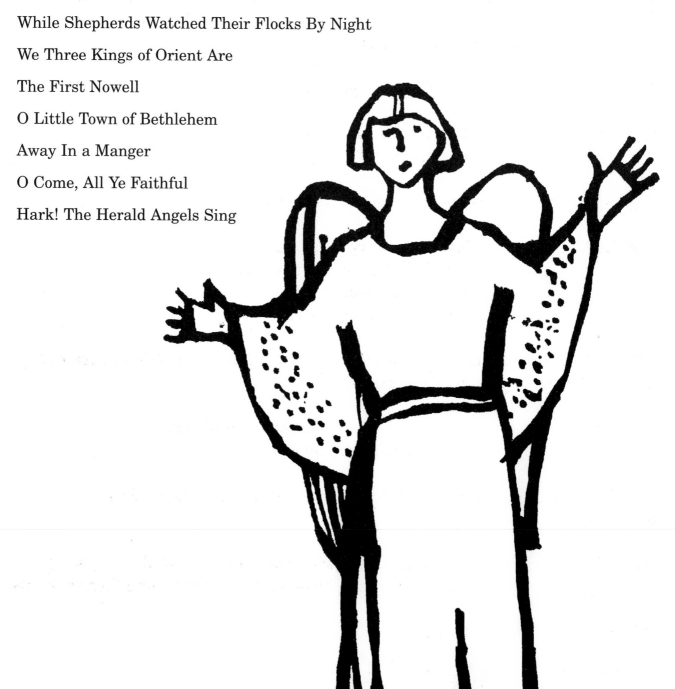

Act 1, Scene 1 – The Nativity Tableau

Inside the Stable. Before the play begins, the actors have assembled on the stage to form the traditional nativity tableau. MARY sits on a stool centre stage, with the baby Jesus in a manger. JOSEPH stands beside her. The THREE KINGS offer their gifts. The SHEPHERDS, the SHEPHERD BOY and their SHEEP gaze at the baby. GABRIEL stands at the back of the group, holding aloft the star on its pole. The ANGELS accompany him. Some COWS and the DONKEY stand nearby. All the actors are very still, as if frozen.

The musical introduction to 'Silent Night' plays.

CHOIR: *(sings)*   Silent night, Holy night,
                                    All is calm, all is bright.

(Lights up. The curtains open. The actors are revealed.)

CHOIR: *(sings)*   'Round yon virgin mother and child
                                    Holy infant so tender and mild
                                    Sleep in heavenly peace,
                                    Sleep in heavenly peace.

(The CHOIR hums another verse of 'Silent Night'. Meanwhile JOSEPH comes to life, leaves the tableau and steps forward.)

JOSEPH: *(to the audience)* Welcome to Bethlehem.
                                    I'm Joseph. A carpenter.

(JOSEPH turns to indicate and introduce the characters in the tableau to the audience.)

JOSEPH: This is Mary, my wife. She's just had a baby.
                                    And these people have come to see him. And these animals.

COWS: Moo!

SHEEP: Baaa!

DONKEY: Neigh!

JOSEPH: *(turning back to the audience)* Looks simple enough.
                           But this baby is special. He will change the world.
                           He is a King. Let us tell you the amazing story of the birth
                           of Jesus Christ. We'll tell you about the three Kings.

(JOSEPH turns to watch as the THREE KINGS come to life and leave the tableau. They exit.)

JOSEPH: *(turning back to the audience)* And the shepherds.

(JOSEPH turns to watch as the SHEPHERDS, the SHEPHERD BOY and the SHEEP come to life and leave the tableau. They exit.)

JOSEPH: *(turning back to the audience)* We'll tell you how
                           Jesus was born not in a royal palace, but in this stable.
                           With no rich carpet on the floor, only straw.
                           We'll tell you about the angels.
                           And the star.

(JOSEPH turns to watch as GABRIEL and the ANGELS come to life and leave the tableau. They exit.)

JOSEPH: *(turning back to the audience)* And why Jesus
                           sleeps not in a comfy cot but in a manger
                           that normally holds the animals' hay.

(He steps to one side.)

                           The story starts with Mary, a little while ago.
                           It starts in Nazareth, in the village where we lived.
                           In Mary's garden...

(The CHOIR stops humming. MARY comes to life and leaves the tableau. She walks forward as if lost in thought. The curtains close behind her and the COWS and the DONKEY exit.)

Act 1, Scene 2 – Gabriel's Visitation

Mary's Garden. JOSEPH stands to one side and watches MARY.

GABRIEL: *(calling from off stage)* Mary! Mary!

(MARY looks around, mystified.)

MARY: Who's there? Who's calling?

(We hear a whooshing noise as GABRIEL enters without the star.)

GABRIEL: I am Gabriel, the Angel of the Lord.

(MARY turns and suddenly sees GABRIEL.)

MARY: *(gasping)* Aaaaaaaah!

(MARY freezes, frightened.)

GABRIEL: *(sings)* Fear not,

CHOIR: *(sings)* Said he
For mighty dread
Had seized her troubled mind.

GABRIEL: *(sings)* Glad tidings of great joy I bring
To you and all mankind.

(The CHOIR hum the tune of 'While Shepherds Watched Their Flocks By Night' as the following conversation takes place.)

GABRIEL: You, Mary, are to have a baby boy.

MARY: *(amazed and shocked)* But I don't understand.
I'm only a girl. I'm not even married yet.

GABRIEL: You are a very special girl, Mary.
God has chosen you to be the mother of His son.

MARY: *(even more amazed)* The son of <u>God</u>?

GABRIEL: Yes. A holy child. And you will take care of Him
                  till He grows up. He will be the promised King.
                  The Saviour of the World.

MARY: But why me?

GABRIEL: God knows how much you love Him.
                  And He loves you, Mary. Will you obey His wishes?

(MARY pauses for a moment, then makes up her mind.)

MARY: I will try. I will do my best.

(GABRIEL smiles and raises his hand.)

GABRIEL: Farewell, Mary. God is with you.

*(The CHOIR stop humming. GABRIEL walks to the back of the stage.
MARY walks a step or two, as if lost in a trance.)*

MARY: Am I dreaming? *(She pinches herself.)*
                  Ow! No, I'm not dreaming! It must be true!
                  It's wonderful! *(She calls excitedly.)* Joseph!

(JOSEPH steps forward into the scene.)

JOSEPH: *(to the audience)* When Mary told me the news,
                  I was very upset. It's not easy to accept that the girl
                  you love is having a child that's not really yours too.

*(MARY'S excitement turns to concern. She looks away as JOSEPH walks sadly
away from her. There is a whooshing noise as GABRIEL walks forward again.
GABRIEL speaks into JOSEPH's ear; JOSEPH does not see him, but hears
his voice.)*

GABRIEL: *(clearly and sincerely)* Joseph! Don't be afraid.
                  Mary hasn't been untrue. She needs you.
                  God needs you both to care for His only son.
                  And Mary needs you to care for her.
                  Believe, Joseph. Believe.

(GABRIEL exits, leaving JOSEPH thinking. MARY looks towards JOSEPH.)

MARY: *(hopefully)* Joseph?

(JOSEPH goes to MARY and puts a protective arm around her.)

JOSEPH: *(firmly)* It's all right, Mary. I believe. I'm with you. I'll be with you all the way.

MARY: *(happy and relieved)* Thank you.

JOSEPH: *(to the audience)* So Mary and I married and waited for the birth of the baby.

(JOSEPH and MARY collect stools from the side of the stage and sit down.)

JOSEPH: Then one day...

Act 1, Scene 3 –
The Roman Soldiers' Proclamation

Mary and Joseph's House. MARY and JOSEPH are sitting on stools. There is a loud knocking sound.

JOSEPH: *(calling)* Come in!

(The FIRST AND SECOND ROMAN SOLDIERS enter. They are very formal. They unroll scrolls and prepare to make an announcement. MARY and JOSEPH stand up nervously and look at the soldiers, waiting for them to speak.)

FIRST SOLDIER: *(reading loudly)* Herod, King of Judea, commands all citizens to travel immediately to their home town.

SECOND SOLDIER: *(reading from his scroll)* All citizens must register their names and pay their taxes!

(The ROMAN SOLDIERS roll up their scrolls, then turn to go. MARY and JOSEPH look at each other in dismay.)

JOSEPH: *(raising his voice)* But our home town is Bethlehem. That's miles away.

FIRST SOLDIER: Can't help that.

SECOND SOLDIER: King Herod says everybody must obey.

(JOSEPH urgently approaches the ROMAN SOLDIERS.)

JOSEPH: *(angrily)* But my wife can't walk that far! She's expecting a baby!

FIRST SOLDIER: *(rudely)* So what? Not our fault.

SECOND SOLDIER: *(with a smirk)* Tell you what! Put her on a donkey!

(The ROMAN SOLDIERS laugh and exit. JOSEPH turns to MARY.)

JOSEPH: *(indignantly)* We can't go all that way!

(MARY joins JOSEPH.)

MARY: *(resigned)* We must, Joseph.

JOSEPH: It's bad enough having to pay taxes to the wretched
                         Romans, let alone having to travel to Bethlehem.
                         You're not strong enough!

(MARY takes JOSEPH's hand.)

MARY: Come on. God will look after us, I'm sure of it.

*(JOSEPH thinks for a moment, then nods in reluctant agreement. MARY smiles
at him and the two exit, as music plays and the CHOIR sings the chorus of
'We Three Kings of Orient Are.' GABRIEL enters, holding aloft the star. He slowly
proceeds halfway to the back of the hall and stops there.)*

CHOIR: *(sings)*   O star of wonder
                         Star of night
                         Star with royal beauty bright
                         Westward leading
                         Still proceeding
                         Guide us to Thy perfect light.

Act 1, Scene 4 –
The Three Kings See the Star

The Kings' Observatory. We hear the loud clash of cymbals, suggesting the Orient. The curtains open. We see a telescope standing centre stage. JOSEPH enters.

JOSEPH: *(to the audience)* A change of scene.
In a distant land, far away in the east...

(The THREE KINGS enter.)

JOSEPH: ...three kings, wise astrologers,
were studying the night sky.

(CASPAR and BALTHAZAR study a chart of the heavens. MELCHIOR scans the sky through the telescope. Suddenly, he sees something.)

MELCHIOR: *(eagerly)* Caspar, Balthazar, look!

(He gestures to CASPAR, who looks through the telescope.)

CASPAR: Saturn is speeding across the sky!

(CASPAR gestures to BALTHAZAR, who looks through the telescope.)

BALTHAZAR: And Jupiter. Like huge comets!
They are heading towards Mars!

(They all look towards the star held by GABRIEL.)

MELCHIOR: What wonder is this? It looks as if Mars,
Jupiter and Saturn have joined together
to make one great big star!

CASPAR: *(suddenly)* It must be a sign, a sign that the new King,
the promised King, is born.

BALTHAZAR: *(eagerly)* Caspar is right. We must follow the star,
find the King and worship Him. Come.

(There is a clash of cymbals. Music plays. The THREE KINGS set off towards the star, singing 'We Three Kings of Orient Are,' as they go. The curtains close behind them.)

KINGS: *(sing)*   We three Kings of Orient are
                           Bearing gifts we traverse afar
                           Field and fountain
                           Moor and mountain
                           Following yonder star.

(GABRIEL moves towards the exit, carrying the star. The THREE KINGS follow.)

KINGS and
CHOIR: *(sing)*   O star of wonder
                           Star of night
                           Star with royal beauty bright
                           Westward leading
                           Still proceeding
                           Guide us to Thy perfect light.

(All exit from the back of the hall.)

Act 1, Scene 5 – While Shepherds Watched

On a Hillside. Lights dim. The curtains open. The SHEEP enter.

SHEEP: Baaa! Baaa! Baaa!

(The CHOIR starts to sing as the SHEPHERDS enter and sit down at the front of the stage. The SECOND SHEPHERD takes a swig from a flask.)

CHOIR: *(sings)*   While shepherds watched
                        Their flocks by night
                        All seated on the ground...

(We hear the menacing beating of a drum. The SECOND SHEPHERD suddenly senses something, sits up and drops his flask.)

FIRST SHEPHERD: What's the matter? A wolf ? *(He looks around.)*

SECOND SHEPHERD: *(as if in a trance)* No, I feel... funny.

FIRST SHEPHERD: It's all that beer you've been drinking.

(The SHEPHERD BOY laughs. He picks up the flask and shakes it.)

SHEPHERD BOY: Yes! Look, you've knocked back a whole flaskful!
                   You greedy hog!

(The FIRST SHEPHERD laughs.)

SECOND SHEPHERD: *(firmly)* No, it's not the beer. Can't you feel it?
                   Something stirring in the air?

FIRST SHEPHERD: You'll be seeing flying sheep next.

(The FIRST SHEPHERD and the SHEPHERD BOY laugh. We hear a whooshing sound. GABRIEL enters without the star.)

CHOIR: *(sings)*   The angel of the Lord came down
                        And glory shone around.

(Lights up.)

FIRST SHEPHERD: Bright green flying sheep!

(The FIRST SHEPHERD and the SHEPHERD BOY rock with laughter. Suddenly the SECOND SHEPHERD turns and sees GABRIEL. He jumps.)

SECOND SHEPHERD: (gasping) Aaaaaaaaah!

(The SHEPHERD BOY turns and sees GABRIEL too. He is terrified.)

SHEPHERD BOY: Help!

FIRST SHEPHERD: Stop mucking about!

(The FIRST SHEPHERD turns round. He sees GABRIEL. He is even more frightened than the other two.)

FIRST SHEPHERD: Aaaaaah! It's a ghost!

ALL: (clinging to each other) Aaaaaaaaaaaaah!

SHEEP: (terrified too) Baaaaaaaaaa!

FIRST SHEPHERD: (fearfully) Who are you?
                              What do you want with us?

GABRIEL: (sings) Fear not,

CHOIR: (sings) Said he,
                              For mighty dread
                              Had seized their troubled minds

GABRIEL: (sings) Glad tidings of great joy I bring   good news
                              To you and all mankind.

(The music continues softly.)

SECOND SHEPHERD: (in awe) Hey! That's no ghost!

SHEPHERD BOY: (whispers) No flying sheep, either!

SECOND SHEPHERD: (amazed) It's an angel!

FIRST SHEPHERD: Hush! Listen!

A saviour is born in Betthehem.
A King.

GABRIEL: *(sings)*   To you in David's town this day
Is born of David's line
A Saviour, who is Christ the Lord
And this shall be the sign:

The heavenly babe you there shall find
To human view displayed
All meanly wrapped in swaddling bands
And in a manger laid.

(Enter the other ANGELS. They stand around GABRIEL.)

CHOIR: *(sings)*   Thus spake the seraph, and forthwith
Appeared a shining throng
Of angels praising God, who thus
Addressed their joyful song:

CHOIR
and ANGELS: *(sing)*   All glory be to God on high
And to the earth be peace;
Goodwill henceforth from heav'n to men
Begin and never cease.

GABRIEL: Go. Worship your King.

(GABRIEL and the ANGELS exit. Or the curtains close in front of them.)

SHEEP: *(nervously)* Baaa! Baaa!

FIRST SHEPHERD: *(thoughtfully)* Quiet, sheep.
The angel said there was nothing to fear.

SHEPHERD BOY: But what does it all mean?

SECOND SHEPHERD: *(excited)* He said the promised King is born.
In the City of David.

In

FIRST SHEPHERD: That's Bethlehem. Here!

SECOND SHEPHERD: Come on, let's find Him.

SHEPHERD BOY: But why us? Why did he come and tell <u>us</u>?

(The FIRST SHEPHERD pauses, then speaks slowly, thinking it through.)

FIRST SHEPHERD: Well, if the King's just been born,
the angels wanted to announce the news.
But it's night-time, so everyone in the town
must be asleep.

SHEPHERD BOY: *(putting two and two together)* We were awake
watching our sheep. So they came and told us!

(The SECOND SHEPHERD jumps up, eager to set off.)

SECOND SHEPHERD: Exactly. We must go and find the King.

SHEPHERD BOY: What, now?

FIRST SHEPHERD: That's what the angel said.

SHEPHERD BOY: But where is He?

SECOND SHEPHERD: In a manger, he said.
Not a cradle or a cot in a royal palace.
In a manger.

(The FIRST SHEPHERD leaps up.)

FIRST SHEPHERD: We'll look in every stable till we find Him!

SHEPHERD BOY: *(hesitantly)* But what about our sheep?
We can't just leave them.

FIRST SHEPHERD: They can come too! Hey, sheep!
Do you want to see the baby King?

SHEEP: Baaaa! Baaaa!

FIRST SHEPHERD: Come on then! Let's go!

(The SHEPHERDS and the SHEEP exit. The SHEPHERDS sing as they go to the tune of 'The First Nowell'.)

SHEPHERDS: *(sing)* Nowell, Nowell, Nowell, Nowell

CHOIR: *(sings)* Born is the King of Israel.

(Enter JOSEPH, MARY and the DONKEY, from the back of the hall.)

JOSEPH: *(talking to the audience as he arrives)*
Mary and I travelled on the long road
to Bethlehem for the tax gathering.
When we were halfway there...

MARY: Joseph, I'm so tired. Couldn't we rest a while?

JOSEPH: Of course, Mary. *(He has an idea.)*
(to the audience) Why don't we all have a rest?
Come back in fifteen minutes' time for the
second half of 'The Christmas Story'.

(JOSEPH and MARY exit. Lights down.)

INTERVAL

Act 2, Prologue – On the Road

Lights up. We hear the clip-clopping of a donkey's hooves. JOSEPH, MARY and the DONKEY enter at the back of the hall.

JOSEPH: *(to the audience)* Mary and I travelled on and on, all day and night, along the dusty road to Bethlehem.

(They walk until they arrive on stage.)

JOSEPH: *(to the audience)* At last the tiring journey was over. We arrived...

(We hear a drum roll.)

Act 2, Scene 1 –
The Tax Gathering in Bethlehem

The Roman Soldiers' Office. The curtains open. We can see a table littered with sheets of paper and feather quill pens. The THIRD AND FOURTH ROMAN SOLDIERS are seated on stools, at the table.

JOSEPH: ...for the tax collection.

MARY: *(weakly)* Joseph, I have to stop. The baby...

JOSEPH: All right, Mary. This shouldn't take long.

(The ROMAN SOLDIERS begin a brusque interrogation.)

THIRD SOLDIER: Name?

JOSEPH: Joseph of Nazareth. This is Mary, my wife.

FOURTH SOLDIER: Occupation?

JOSEPH: Carpenter.

THIRD SOLDIER: Own house?

JOSEPH: Yes, I built it myself.

FOURTH SOLDIER: Paid for?

JOSEPH: Almost. I borrowed the money.
                    I'm paying it back as fast as I can.

THIRD SOLDIER: How much did you earn last year?

JOSEPH: Four thousand talents.

(MARY feels very weak. She crouches down.)

MARY: Joseph, please...

JOSEPH: Nearly finished, Mary.

FOURTH SOLDIER: Any animals? What's the matter with her?

MARY: *(bravely)* It's all right. I'm exhausted.
                    The journey.

FOURTH SOLDIER: Animals?

(JOSEPH looks over to MARY with concern.)

JOSEPH: Just the donkey. Please hurry.

THIRD SOLDIER: Any fig orchards?

FOURTH SOLDIER: Olive groves?

THIRD SOLDIER: Vineyards?

JOSEPH: No.

MARY: *(in pain)* Joseph!

JOSEPH: Please let us go; my wife's about to have a baby.

FOURTH SOLDIER: *(almost kindly)* Really?
Why didn't you tell us before?

THIRD SOLDIER: *(fiercely)* That affects your tax.

FOURTH SOLDIER: *(working it out)* That'll be... six hundred talents.

(JOSEPH pays money to the FOURTH SOLDIER. MARY collapses, exhausted. JOSEPH rushes to her side.)

THIRD SOLDIER: She looks rough.

JOSEPH: Please, is there anywhere we can stay?

THIRD SOLDIER: Don't ask me. I don't live here.

FOURTH SOLDIER: *(showing a spark of humanity)* There's an inn over the road. You could try there.

(He points to the other side of the stage.)

JOSEPH: Thank you. Let's go, Mary.
Hold on to me.

THIRD SOLDIER: *(shouts)* Next!

(JOSEPH starts to help MARY across the stage.)

(The ROMAN SOLDIERS exit, or the curtains close in front of them.)

JOSEPH: *(to the audience)*
Well, we tried the inn.
We tried lots of inns.
But the answer was always the same.

(JOSEPH and MARY pause. JOSEPH looks up. One by one the INNKEEPERS enter and say their lines, building to a nightmarish climax.)

FIRST INNKEEPER: You can't stay here!

SECOND INNKEEPER: We're full up!

THIRD INNKEEPER: Clear off!

FOURTH INNKEEPER: No room!

FIFTH INNKEEPER: No room!

ALL INNKEEPERS: <u>NO ROOM!</u>

(The INNKEEPERS exit.)

JOSEPH: It's hopeless, Mary.

MARY: Please, Joseph. We must keep trying. We must find somewhere. The baby's nearly here.

(MARY and JOSEPH exit.)

Act 2, Scene 2 – No Room at the Inn

Outside the Tavern. The curtains open. We see an inn sign. It reads 'Bethlehem Tavern'. Off stage, we can hear the raucous voices of folk drinking in the tavern, followed by riotous laughter, as though someone has told a funny joke. Then lines are called out at random, as if from the numerous merrymakers inside the tavern. We hear the sound of glasses chinking. As this is going on, MARY and JOSEPH enter.

FIRST VOICE: Innkeeper, more ale!

SECOND VOICE: Coming sir!

THIRD VOICE: Barnabas, long time no see!

FOURTH VOICE: How are you?

FIFTH VOICE: *(drunkenly)* Give me another drink!

SECOND VOICE: I think you've had enough, sir!

(JOSEPH mimes pulling a bell rope. We hear the ringing of the bell. The LAST INNKEEPER and the INNKEEPER'S WIFE enter. The off stage hubbub continues, but the volume decreases to allow the following conversation to be heard.)

INNKEEPER'S WIFE: *(cross, because she is so busy)* Yes?

JOSEPH: Please. Have you a room for the night?

LAST INNKEEPER: You must be joking.

INNKEEPER'S WIFE: Everyone's pouring in for the tax gathering.

LAST INNKEEPER: We're packed to the rafters.

JOSEPH: We're desperate. My wife is having a baby.

INNKEEPER'S WIFE: What a time to choose! I'd like to help, but...

LAST INNKEEPER:	Most of our guests are Roman soldiers; they're not likely to give up their rooms.
MARY:	Please...
JOSEPH:	We've tried everywhere!
INNKEEPER'S WIFE:	*(to her husband)* What about that stable round the back?
JOSEPH:	*(not sure)* A stable?
MARY:	Thank you. That'll be fine.
LAST INNKEEPER:	But it's where we keep the animals!
MARY:	Anywhere. Please.
INNKEEPER'S WIFE:	Come on, then.

(As the music begins for 'O Little Town of Bethlehem' the LAST INNKEEPER and the INNKEEPER'S WIFE lead MARY and JOSEPH off stage. Lights dim.)

Act 2, Scene 3 – Jesus is Born

Inside the Stable. There is a stool in the stable. The COWS enter as the CHOIR sing the first verse of 'O Little Town of Bethlehem.'

CHOIR: *(sings)* O little town of Bethlehem
How still we see thee lie!
Above thy deep and dreamless sleep
The silent stars go by.
Yet in thy dark streets shineth
The everlasting light.
The hopes and fears of all the years
Are met in thee tonight.

COWS: Moo! Moo!

(Enter the LAST INNKEEPER and the INNKEEPER'S WIFE. They lead MARY, JOSEPH and the DONKEY into the stable.)

LAST INNKEEPER: It's not luxury, as you might say, but it's warm
and I changed the straw myself this morning.

INNKEEPER'S WIFE: Take no notice of the animals.
They're used to human company.

JOSEPH: Thank you. You're very kind.

(MARY sits on the stool. The COWS and DONKEY surround her, hiding her from view.)

INNKEEPER'S WIFE: Just don't let on you're here to anyone else.
Don't want any more riff raff clamouring
to get in for the night!

LAST INNKEEPER: And don't leave any litter either.
'Night.

(The LAST INNKEEPER and the INNKEEPER'S WIFE exit.)

JOSEPH: *(to the audience)* So, in this stable,
the baby Jesus was born.

(A baby's cry is heard. JOSEPH fetches the manger with the baby in it. He brings it to MARY. MARY, concealed by the COWS and the DONKEY, takes the baby from the manger.)

JOSEPH: We laid Him not in a proper crib, but in a manger.

(The COWS and the DONKEY move to reveal MARY. She lays the baby in the manger.)

CHOIR: *(sings)*   Away in a manger, no crib for a bed
The little Lord Jesus laid down His sweet head.
The stars in the bright sky looked down where He lay,
The little Lord Jesus asleep in the hay.

The cattle are lowing, the baby awakes,
But little Lord Jesus, no crying He makes...

(The CHOIR quietly hum the tune of the last two lines of the verse, as MARY picks up the baby, gently rocks Him to sleep on her lap, then puts Him back in the manger.)

Act 2, Scene 4 – The Travellers Arrive

Inside the Stable. From the back of the hall we hear the voice of GABRIEL, singing the first verse of 'O Come, All Ye Faithful'. He carries his star and leads the other ANGELS, the KINGS, the SHEPHERDS and the SHEEP towards the stable, as the carol continues.

GABRIEL: *(sings)*   O come, all ye faithful
   Joyful and triumphant
   Come ye O come ye
   To Bethlehem

ALL: *(sing)*   Come and behold Him
   Born the King of Angels:

   O come, let us adore Him
   O come, let us adore Him
   O come, let us adore Him
   Christ the Lord.

   God of God
   Light of Light
   Lo, he abhors not
   The Virgin's womb
   Very God
   Begotten not created

   O come, let us adore Him
   O come, let us adore Him
   O come, let us adore Him
   Christ the Lord.

(By the end of the carol, everyone has arrived and grouped themselves around the manger. The KINGS step forward and reverently present their gifts.)

KINGS: The new King is born.
   Praise be to God.

CASPAR: We bring Him gifts. Precious gold.

BALTHAZAR: Sweet-smelling frankincense.

MELCHIOR: And healing myrrh.

(They position themselves in the tableau. The SHEPHERDS step forward.)

BOTH SHEPHERDS: God bless the Christ Child.

FIRST SHEPHERD: May He bring peace to the world.

SECOND SHEPHERD: And joy to all men.

SHEPHERD BOY: And all shepherd boys!

SHEEP: Baaaaa!

SHEPHERD BOY: And all sheep!

MARY: Thank you. Thank you all.

SHEPHERD BOY: What's His name?

MARY: Jesus.

SHEPHERD BOY: Is He really a King?

FIRST SHEPHERD: Course He is!

SECOND SHEPHERD: Didn't the angel say so?

SHEPHERD BOY: But why wasn't He born in a royal palace?

MARY: If He was born in a posh palace,
                  it might look as if He's only interested in posh people.

JOSEPH: I think He was born in a poor stable because
                  God wanted to show us that this King isn't proud.
                  He loves everyone. Posh and poor alike.

MARY: And hopefully everyone will love Him and believe in Him.

SHEPHERD BOY: *(looking in the manger)* I believe in you, Jesus.

SHEPHERDS
and KINGS: We <u>all</u> believe in you, Jesus.

SHEEP: *(nodding)* Baaaaa!

(JOSEPH steps forward a little.)

JOSEPH: *(to the audience)* So there we are:
                              we've told you the Christmas story.
                              And this is the end.

SHEPHERD BOY: The end? I reckon this is just the beginning!

(The music begins as JOSEPH steps back into the tableau, which is now complete. Everyone sings the first verse of 'Hark! The Herald Angels Sing'.)

ALL: *(sing)*   Hark! The herald angels sing
                           Glory to the new-born King,
                           Peace on earth, and mercy mild,
                           God and sinners reconciled.
                           Joyful, all ye nations, rise,
                           Join the triumph of the skies;
                           With the angelic host proclaim,
                           'Christ is born in Bethlehem'.

                           Hark! The herald angels sing
                           Glory to the new-born King.

(The actors hold their positions for a moment. As the audience starts applauding, the actors, choir and musicians all take a bow, followed by the stage management team. Lights dim, as the curtains close.)

THE END

Staging

Area for Performance

You could certainly perform individual scenes from *The Christmas Story* at the front of a classroom. But in order to stage the full-length play you will need more space than that. School halls do vary widely, but there are different ways in which you can create the right kind of space for the actors and the choir.

Making the action visible to everyone in the audience will be your main concern. If you have a stage, that will certainly help, but a platform made of rostra blocks will work well too. Moreover, the action needn't be restricted to the stage area alone. You could designate an acting area in front of the stage or platform, at floor level. Steps should lead down from the stage or platform to the floor, so that the actors can move from one area to the other. The choir and percussion instrumentalists should sit to one side, so that they can see the accompanist or conductor.

You will find that there are directions for the use of stage curtains within the playscript. But if you do not have curtains, nor a raised stage or platform, don't worry! These things are not essential. If your acting area is all on the same level, some scenes can take place at the front of that area (downstage) and other scenes further back (upstage). If you don't have curtains, the stage management team can make scene changes in view of the audience.

Access to the acting area can be created in different ways. A stage will probably have wings and a door leading backstage. Or, if you are using the school hall, there will be classrooms or corridors at either end of the hall. The actors can assemble at the stage end of the hall and enter from the sides or assemble behind the audience and enter down the aisle. Gabriel can lead the processions to and from the stage along the central or side aisles.

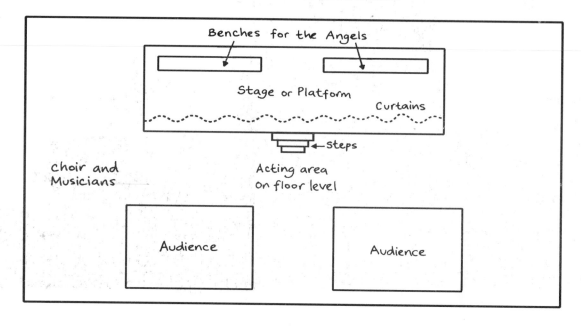

Staging

Backdrops

The basic setting for the play should be as simple as possible. At the back of the performance area there could be a bare, painted wall, or curtains, or a backdrop. Black, grey or dark blue would be the most suitable colours. If you have time and the resources to make a backdrop (and a helpful art department!) it could show a night sky with the silhouetted shapes of houses in the distance. This would be appropriate for all scenes.

However, if you would like to have several backdrops and have the facilities to change them, then I would suggest that you might make three: to show a stable interior, a night sky and a street in Bethlehem. This would cover you for all the scenes in the play! Another option, if your head teacher will allow this, is to paint a suitable mural on the wall behind the stage. (This can be painted over afterwards.) But a bare wall behind the stage is perfectly acceptable.

Scenery and Props

The Christmas Story has been written with the intention that the basic settings should be as simple as possible, so that scene changes can take place quickly and easily. There are nine scenes and a prologue in *The Christmas Story*. There are seven different locations, but most of these only require a minimum of scenery and some none at all. There are several small props which the actors will carry (see Small Props) but most of them are easy to find or make.

Inside the Stable

Three scenes from the play take place in this location. The nativity tableau in the first and last scenes of the play makes its own setting. All that is necessary is a stool for Mary to sit on, and a manger. A folding wooden washing up rack, covered with a piece of cloth, is just the right shape for the manger. Alternatively, you could use a rectangular cardboard box. Paint the shape of the manger on the outside. Put a couple of pillows inside it, and place the doll representing baby Jesus on top of them.

Mary and Joseph's House

All that is required is a couple of stools for the two to sit on.

The Kings' Observatory

All that you need to show the audience the observatory is a telescope. Ideally, this should be on a stand. To make this, first borrow a music stand from the music department. Fold down the music rack. Then, find a wide cardboard roll (at least 40cm long and 10cm in diameter). Paint it black and decorate it with some gold stars. Tape it securely to the folded-down music rack at each end of the tube. Tilt your telescope up towards the sky. Alternatively, a hand-held telescope can be passed from one actor to another.

Mary's Garden

No scenery is needed at all.

On a Hillside

No special scenery is wanted for this scene – the sheep provide atmosphere!

Scenery and Props

The Roman Soldiers' Office
Their office is furnished with a small table and two stools for them to sit on. On the table, there should be a pile of paper scrolls and some feather quills for pens.

Outside the Tavern
You will require a sign for the local inn. You could paint its name – 'Bethlehem Tavern' – on to a square piece of old sheet (100 cm by 100cm) and suspend this at the back of the stage. Or you might like to staple the material at the top, around a piece of dowling, about 120cm long. Two actors or members of the stage management team could hold up the sign during the short scene.

Or you could make a smaller sign from paper and attach it to a pole. One person could display it from the wings.

The Star
Gabriel carries the star on a pole. Make the star itself about 15cm in diameter. Cut it out of cardboard and paint it gold. Glue on some glitter too. Make a hole at the edge of one of the star's points. Use a piece of dowling or a broom handle for the pole. Thread the star on to some string, make a small loop, then wrap the ends of the string around the pole and fasten them with a knot. Secure it at the end of the pole with tape.

Small Props

The actors will need to carry some props themselves. They should know what their props are, and collect them from the props tables, before the beginning of each act. These props are:

Act 1, Scene 1
Glittery boxes for the Three Kings to give to baby Jesus (and in Act 2, sc. 4)
Act 1, Scene 1
The star on its pole for Gabriel (and in Act 1, sc. 4 and Act 2, sc. 4)
Act 1, Scene 3
Two scrolls for the Roman Soldiers
Act 1, Scene 5
Crooks for all the Shepherds
A flask for the Second Shepherd
Act 2, Scene 1
A money bag for Joseph
Act 2, Scene 3
The doll representing baby Jesus for Mary

Lighting

It would be possible to perform the play with no special lighting at all. Most performances will be in daytime, when natural light will be enough.

But if you have some stage lighting it is worth using it to add theatricality to your production. There are some specific lighting suggestions in the script, which you can follow. You could also draw the blinds or curtains to cut out the natural daylight.

Arrange good general coverage lighting for the acting areas and allow enough light for the choir and musicians to be visible.

Make sure that Joseph can be seen clearly, whenever he is addressing the audience. You might like to use small fairy-type lights to suggest stars in the Shepherds' scene. They could be strung across the backcloth of the night sky, looking almost invisible until they are turned on.

If you have no special lighting at all, don't worry! Turn the hall lights off before the audience arrive, then turn them on just before the play starts, to let them know something is about to happen. Turn them off for the interval, and then back on again for Act 2.

Casting and Auditions

Casting the Parts

This needs to be done quite tactfully. Asking the children which parts they would like to play could prove fatal, as many of the children may feel that they would like a starring role!

I suggest that you start by talking to them about the story of the play. You could show them the illustrations of the characters on pages 40 - 43, and give them an idea of the general atmosphere of the play; tell them that the story took place long ago, but the characters are in many ways just like people are today. Then let them show off their skills with a few drama exercises! (There are some games and exercises suggested overleaf.) You could make firm decisions after that.

Some of the roles are quite challenging, and you will need to find an actor to play Joseph who is comfortable speaking directly to the audience. Gabriel should be a good singer. Mary has to display a strong and gutsy character. If you decide to use younger children to play angels and sheep, it's a good idea to let the uninhibited ones play sheep. Entering on your knees and baaing on cue can be quite intimidating!

Let the children know that there are interesting alternatives to acting; such as working on the stage management team. Everyone should be encouraged to take the whole thing seriously; but assure them it will be fun too!

Casting and Auditions

Group Auditions

Formal auditions are perhaps not appropriate for this age group. I would suggest that a series of drama exercises and games will give you the information that you need to help you cast the parts, without being too intimidating a process for the children!

• First of all, you could try some movement games like musical statues. You will soon be able to see who has good co-ordination and can concentrate.

• You could suggest that the children pretend to be particular characters. Ask them to show you how the Kings walk, how the Roman Soldiers march, and how an animal walks, stretches and goes to sleep.

• Make them work in pairs to play the 'mirror game'. They should face each other. One starts by miming an action suggested by you, such as cleaning his or her teeth. The other has to follow the movements as closely as possible, as if looking in a mirror. Talking and giggling forbidden! This is harder than it sounds, and the children who take this seriously will be able to cope with the discipline of playing a bigger role.

• Ask everyone to choose a character or an animal. They set off round the hall as if they are 'on the way to Bethlehem'. At verbal cues, the children, in character, mime crossing a stream, climbing over a wall or stopping for a meal.

After that, you could ask the keenest and most able actors to try some more sophisticated improvisation. They could work in groups.

• Ask them to show you the Kings studying the stars, and then the moment when they see *the* star, or to show you the Shepherds relaxing on the hillside, and then suddenly seeing Gabriel.

Look for the children who are enjoying acting in this way, and who can convey excitement or fear. You will be able to see which children have a natural presence and might best play the larger roles.

Emphasize to the children how important *everybody's* role is, no matter how large or small. Encourage the children for whom acting has no appeal to be members of the stage management team, or to join the choir or the musicians. In this way, you can include everyone who wants to take part in the production!

The Characters

Mary
Sensitive, but practical too.
The journey shows her courage
and faith.

Joseph
The narrator. An honest
and plain-spoken carpenter.
Loyal and protective.

**Caspar, Melchior and Balthazar
The Three Kings**
They have a regal air and natural
authority. This contrasts with their
eager enthusiasm for star-gazing.

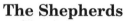

The Shepherds
Good humoured and fond of a joke,
but God-fearing too.

The Shepherd Boy
Lively, bright and a bit
cheeky. Has a serious
and thoughtful side.

Sheep
Very vocal. These sheep
make their feelings known.
They tend to do the same
thing at the same time.

Gabriel
An archangel with
a commanding presence.

Angels
Very dignified with radiant smiles.
They are definitely bringing good news.

The Characters

Cows
Gentle and welcoming.
Slow-moving.

Donkey
Uncomplaining
and loyal.

The Roman Soldiers in Nazareth
Full of their own power and importance.
Impatient and unkind.

The Roman Soldiers in Bethlehem
Sharp. To the point. Business-like.

The Innkeepers
Overworked and short-tempered.

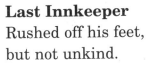

Last Innkeeper
Rushed off his feet,
but not unkind.

Innkeeper's Wife
Busy and sharp-tongued
on the surface. But she
has a good heart.

The Stage Management Team

Tell the children that the role of the stage management team is an essential one, and that their contribution is as important as that of the actors or the choir. They will have some interesting and creative jobs to do.

These include being in charge of the props table, or helping with the lighting. Some of the jobs need a degree of supervision, but as much responsibility as possible should be given to the children involved.

Lighting
An adult will be required to supervise if theatrical lighting is used, but he or she will certainly need an assistant! If you are using ordinary lights in the hall, one person could turn them on and off at appropriate moments.

Operating the Curtains
If you have stage curtains, then two people could be in charge of operating them, following the stage directions within their copy of the playscript, which should be marked with their cues.

Props Table
Two people are needed to organise two props tables, one on each side of the stage. They should check that all the props are there before the performance and hand them out to the actors.

Front of House
Others could organise the seating for the choir and the audience, usher the audience to their seats, and hand out the programmes.

Prompter
The prompter will sit off stage, with a copy of the playscript, alert and ready to remind the actors of their lines, should they forget them!

Scene Shifters
Members of the team should be in charge of putting up backdrops, and carrying pieces of scenery and props on and off. They could also display the tavern sign.

Tidying Up!
Everyone should tidy up afterwards - including the actors and the choir!

Rehearsal Schedule

It's a good idea to work out a clear rehearsal schedule, with the children involved organised into different groups. This means you won't keep too many children hanging around with nothing to do. The choir and musicians can have separate rehearsals. Divide the play into sections and only call the actors you need to rehearse.

As the day of the performance approaches, the children will enjoy putting all the sections together and seeing what the others have been rehearsing and feel the excitement of adding in the singing and the sound effects.

Costume

Most children find dressing up fun. Teachers should time the costume fittings and dress rehearsals carefully. They can inject a much-needed burst of fresh enthusiasm into the actors! The costumes for this play are quite straightforward. Perhaps you can beg or borrow some items of clothing from the children's parents, such as nightshirts or leggings. These can be used for several different costumes. All the characters (except the Three Kings and the animals) should wear leather sandals, if possible.

Even better, maybe some of the parents or other teachers would be willing to help make the costumes. Establish some basic designs first; in this way you can ensure that the Roman Soldiers look as though they come from the same legion!

Although the roles have been listed as male, female and unisex in this section, there is no reason why any of the roles shouldn't be played by children of either sex. Designate the roles in the way that suits your production.

Female Roles

Mary

Mary requires a simple full-length blue or white dress. If you can't beg or borrow one, you could make a simple shift dress for her. You can use the pattern shown on the right to make the costumes for several other characters as well, if you wish to do so.

This pattern gives sample measurements, but you should adapt them to fit the individual actor.

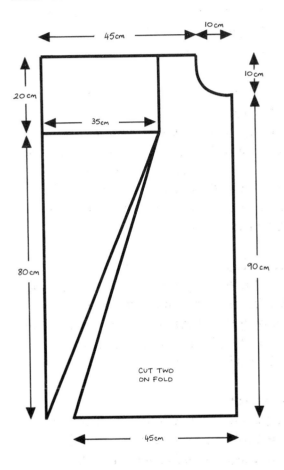

You will need fabric at least 115cm wide, in order to cut out the dress in one piece. Fold your piece of material, so that you have a double thickness, with the fold on the right-hand side. Cut out two of the shapes shown above from the material. Unfold them and lay them on top of each other. Sew up along the sides and the sleeves. You could hem the cuffs, neck and bottom edge of the dress, or leave them ragged. Mary could wear a shawl.

Innkeeper's Wife

She needs a long dress in a natural colour, plus a shawl.

Costume

Male Roles

Joseph

Joseph could wear a long shift, similar to Mary's, in brown or cream. Or it might be fun to dress him in a long striped nightshirt (with rolled up sleeves) and trousers or leggings underneath.
Give him a carpenter's apron as well.

Last Innkeeper

He could also wear a long striped shirt and trousers, or a simple tunic. (A tunic can be made using Mary's dress pattern.) He could wear a long apron. The other innkeepers can be similarly dressed.

Gabriel

You will see that the pattern for Mary's dress may also be used to make an angel's costume with long flowing sleeves, to suggest wings. Alternatively, he could wear a long white nightshirt, decorated with gold paper stars! Use gold tinsel to make him a comfortable halo.

Fasten it with hair pins.

The Three Kings

Oversized white shirts and dark-coloured leggings or trousers (rolled up at the knee) form the basis of their costumes. To show their grandeur, they should wear brightly-coloured cloaks and crowns. An opulent-looking piece of material, such as an old brocade curtain, will make an excellent cloak. Thread the piece of material through with ribbon to make a drawstring for the neck of the cloak. The Kings could wear slippers on their feet, decorated with pom-poms, or ribbon.

Their crowns are easy to make. Cut out a 30cm wide and 60cm long strip of thin gold card. Cut eight spikes into it.

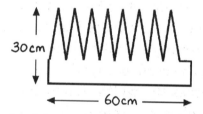

Fit the crown to the actor's head, and staple the ends together. Fold all its spikes outwards and glue or staple them on to the headband. Decorate the crown with foil-covered chocolate coins.

One of the Kings could wear a turban, made from a colourful, glittery scarf; wind it around the actor's head, then tuck in the ends.

Costume

The Shepherds and Shepherd Boy

Large striped shirts or nightshirts make good shepherds' smocks. They should be worn over dark leggings or trousers (corduroy trousers would be very appropriate). A simple headdress will look effective. First, tie two nylon pop socks together, to make a circular band. Then lay a tea towel on the actor's head. Use the band to secure the tea towel in place. Tuck the part of the headdress on the actor's forehead into the band.

The Roman Soldiers

The Roman Soldiers could wear white tunics with breastplates on top. (You could make the tunics from an old sheet. Adapt the pattern on page 45 to make the tunics knee-length.) You can make a breastplate from corrugated cardboard. Cut out a rectangle (100cm long by 35cm wide) from the cardboard, with the ridges running across the width. Remove a circle of cardboard (18cm in diameter) from the middle of the rectangle, to make an opening for the actor's head. You could paint a Roman symbol on the front!

You could make them helmets too.

Unisex Roles

Angels

You can use the pattern on page 45 to make long-sleeved costumes for the angels. Or, they could wear white nightdresses or nightshirts, and silver tinsel haloes.

The Donkey

The actor playing the donkey should wear a grey long-sleeved top and leggings. You could make a mask for the donkey using the template below. Fold all the strips at the back and staple them together. This mask sits on top of the actor's head. Fasten elastic to go under the chin.

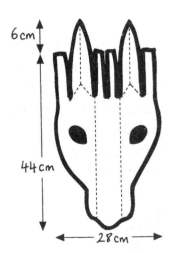

The Sheep

The actors playing the sheep could wear black, white, brown or grey tracksuits. They could have white paper chain tails!

The Cows

The costumes could be white or brown, with spots cut out from adhesive-backed plastic stuck on them. The actors could wear masks too. All the actors playing animals should wear trainers or gym shoes.

Music

The choir sing the carols and the Christmas hymns, and also hum the tunes as 'underscoring' in several scenes, to create atmosphere. A teacher could accompany the choir on the piano or guitar. Or the music for the carols can be played by the school orchestra.

If the actor playing Gabriel has a strong singing voice, he can sing his lines as solos. But he may feel more confident if the choir accompanies him.

Sound Effects

You will notice that the cast list includes the sound effects makers – or percussion instrumentalists. This play requires sound effects at various points, indicated in the stage directions. Almost all the sound effects can be made using percussion instruments.

A whooshing noise = play the xylophone

A loud knock at the door = strike a woodblock

A sound of the Orient = strike a gong or cymbal

To create tension = play the drums

Horses' hooves = knock flowerpots or half-coconut shells together

Ringing the bell at the Inn = ring a handbell

Glasses chinking = knock chunky beer tankards together (not too hard!)

You might like to incorporate other simple keyboard sounds, or to use triangles and woodblocks to make other sound effects. The choir might also augment the animal noises!

And Finally...

Try to enjoy it! Your enthusiasm for the production will be infectious and encourage the children to do their very best. Sometimes rehearsals will feel like wading through treacle! But it is amazing how children rise to the big occasion and make all the hard work worthwhile. And be assured they will never forget the challenge and the excitement of their first theatrical experience.

Happy Christmas, everyone!